Trusting Soul

Volume 6: Collected Stories & Drawings of Brian Andreas

StoryPeople
Decorah

ISBN 0-9642660-6-7

The people in this book, if at one time real, are now entirely fictitious, having been subjected to a combination of a selective memory and a fertile imagination. Any resemblance to real people you might know, even if they are the author's relatives, is entirely coincidental, and is a reminder that you are imagining the incidents in this book as much as the author is.

StoryPeople
P.O. Box 7
Decorah, IA 52101
USA
319.382.8060
319.382.0263 FAX
800.476.7178

storypeople@storypeople.com
www.storypeople.com

First Edition: October, 2000

Printed by the West Coast Print Center, Oakland, California

To my sons, David Quinn & Matthew Shea, for the immense gifts of spirit & strength & creativity they bring to this world we call home

& always, to Ellen, for the bright light of her love & her exquisite way of calling forth extraordinary lives from everyone she touches

Other books by Brian Andreas available
from StoryPeople Press:

Cover Art: Brian Andreas
Back photo: Jon Duder

Trusting Soul

Introduction

My working title for this book was 'The Roaring Dance', from a story that went like this: feeling every cell of her body, roaring & dancing & laughing. As I sorted the stories, I kept that in mind, how each one of these stories burst with the pleasure of simply being alive. But somehow, the stories had their own idea. They asked me to take another look at what these past two years had been & how they had transformed me. They showed me how often I had looked uncertainly into the future & how often that future had unfolded perfectly, though not always without a bit of uncomfortable stretching. They kept whispering of trust & intention & choice. Along the way, I never saw it. But after spending weeks with all these stories, it came clear to me: while I love being alive a whole lot, I also like to keep one eye peeled for danger. Even if I have to make it up, so I won't have wasted all that time peeling.

I had my reasons. We all do. Mine was my family. I had myself convinced that if I could prevent enough of the possible crises that come with having two children, that we'd all be safe & dry & warm & our lives would be perfect. It was easy when they were younger. We covered the electric sockets & had them wear bike helmets three times the size of their heads & made them chew every bite fifty times. But as they grew up & went out into the world on their own, it became much more subtle & difficult & constant. Does an R-rated movie lead to lasting psychic damage? What about too much Disney? What do you do about groundwater contamination? How do you get kids to eat more roughage? It felt like I was playing some weird game with an opponent who never slept & kept switching sides without warning.

Then suddenly, or maybe not so suddenly, but inevitably, I understood that there is one thing you cannot prevent & it's the same for all of us, whether we have children or not. It's called life

& no matter how we plan & barricade & outline with bright yellow safety paint, life itself remains inherently dangerous & unpredictable. Somewhere along the way, I had forgotten that simple fact.

But the stories didn't. They reminded me that the future arrives whether I like it or not. It comes of its own accord & pays little attention to my wishes. They pointed out, ever so gently, that the future is what you bring with you & it's very easy in this wildly heaving & panting world of ours to bring along things you really have no need of: fear & hatred & greed & doubt & on & on.

I think that's it, after all. The future is what you bring with you & you get to choose. I think of the stories & drawings in this book as the things I have chosen, the suitcase I've packed for the future. It's only the essentials, because I know you'll bring stuff, too. I packed the lilt of a voice, the curve of a neck in laughter, the glance between people who have wrapped up in each other in the soft night. I've put in memories of my grandparents & other made-up people because it seemed like they'd be fun to have around. I've thrown in more than enough packages of love & play & chocolate because the future can always use extra of those & I sneaked in a few unexpected gifts, simply because there is no greater joy than an unexpected gift to a trusting soul.

In fact, you could consider this book packed full of gifts for the future. Gifts of laughter & silliness. Of questions that quite possibly have no answer. Of moments that tie together in a net that will always catch you, whether you believe it or not. The future is what you bring with you & this is what I've brought. I know it's enough to at least get us started…

With love,

Brian Andreas
On Matthew's birthday
16 October 2000

the hardest thing
is listening well
enough to quit
worrying about
dying

Is there a lot of stuff
you don't understand?
she said & I said pretty
much the whole thing
& she nodded & said
that's what she thought,
but it was nice to hear
it anyway & we sat there
in the porch swing,
listening to the wind
& growing up together,

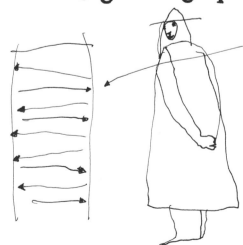

doorway that only
lets some stuff
through but you never
know what it's going
to choose, so it's
hard to plan for the
future

gathering up bits of the world

& setting them out in an order that her children CAN understand

I tell stories for very good reasons, she said, but I'm not going to tell you what they are

or you'd start reading too much in to them

Good Reasons

I can remember walking down the street, saying my name over & over, until all of a sudden, it didn't sound like my name anymore. It didn't even sound like a word at all & then I stopped & the silence rushed in & whispered words that sounded more like my real name & I smiled

& thought to myself how surprised my parents would be when they found out what a mistake they had made.

HELLO! My name is ~~Clapping~~

Real Name

1   1006   92   53 4/1   10096

IMPARTIAL
JUDGE
unless there
are treats
involved

The problem with
knowing everything's
going exactly as it
needs to is that when
you're not having
that much fun it doesn't
even do any good
to complain.

fast forwarding
through her
messages
hoping to
hear from old boyfriends
who finally realize the treasure they've thrown away

Partial Enlightenment

getting ready to jump as high as
she can just because there's
only so long you can sit
politely & listen while
people talk

about
any
old
stuff that
comes in to
their heads

I finally got to
exactly where I
wanted to be, she
said, so why won't
all these growth
experiences go away
& leave me alone?

Pesky Growth

I used to be pretty clear, on what was real & what I made up, but with everything going on in the world, none of that seems to matter, so I just decided to talk less & smile to myself more, so as not to add to the general confusion.

It's hard to believe anything I say, she told me, because I was there & I have a vested interest in being right.

General Confusion

I'm of the opinion that people
don't know what they're talking
about 90 percent of the time,
my grandpa said & my grandma
smiled & said, O, you're too
late. The 10 percent slot filled
up a few minutes ago.

    & we could hear him
    muttering all the way
    back out to the garden

If I had it to do all over again, he told me, I'd
probably do it
the same
way.

But I wouldn't
tell your grand-
mother about it.

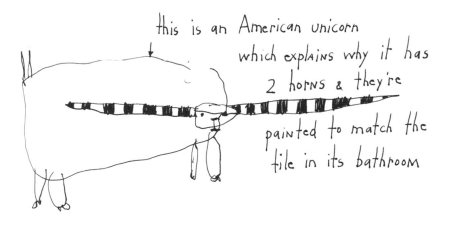

this is an American unicorn which explains why it has 2 horns & they're painted to match the tile in its bathroom

I try to use
unconditional love
in small amounts,
she said, so people
really appreciate it.

The rest of the time
I just try not to yell.

Unconditional Love

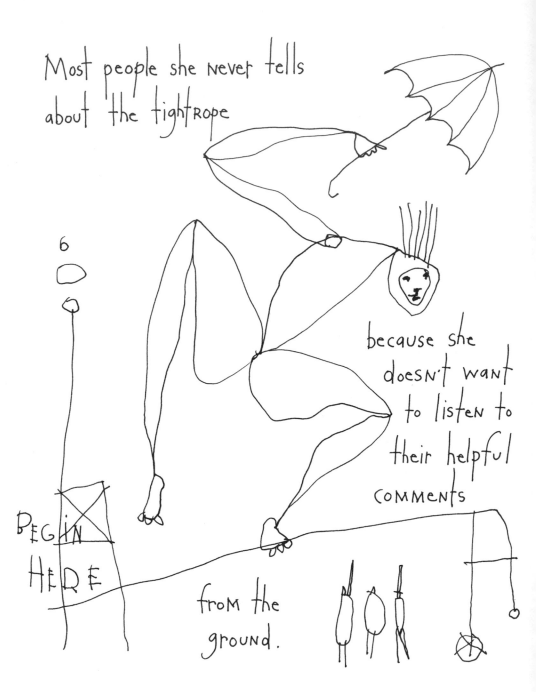

Most people she never tells
about the tightrope

6

because she
doesn't want
to listen to
their helpful
comments

BEGIN
HERE

from the
ground.

Tightrope

The thing about money is you can't think about it too much, he told me, or you won't sleep at night & you get dark circles under your eyes & nothing seems fun any more. I told him it was that way with a lot of things & he nodded & said, yeah, but with money it makes sense.

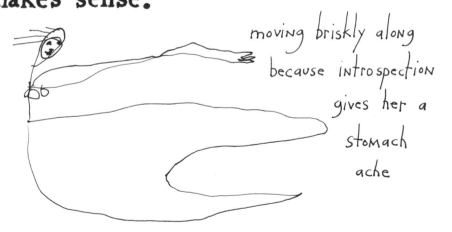

moving briskly along because introspection gives her a stomach ache

Sometimes I think we should bury all our money in a hole & go back to enjoying life again, he said. It'd probably be a good idea to make a map of where the hole was just in case it didn't work out though.

cave filled with stuff that people will kill foR, which oNly goes to show you how confused people are about important things

Backup Plan

feeding anything
that looks even
vaguely fierce
since he
doesn't feel
like dealing
with that
kind of
stuff today

I'm a good jumper, he said,
but I'm not so good at landing.
Maybe you should stay closer
to the ground then, I said & he
shook his head & said the ground
was the whole problem in the
first place.

Good Jumper

this was supposed to be just like the Trojan Horse except all they had was enough wood for the legs & an old wool blanket & the funny thing is it still worked because everyone came out & pointed at it & laughed themselves sick

Don't you dare be rational at a time like this, she told me, or I'll be forced to admit I wasted all these years on you.

Ultimatum

She learned to love him before
he thought it was even possible,
so he didn't have a chance to
hide & mess it up & while it
was a little scary at times,
mainly he could not even imagine
the world without her there

these are multiple shadows because there
were a lot of things she walked away from
without a word of
explanation when she
was younger
& she still
thinks about
them
more than
she needs to

Possible Love

I'm feeling overdressed,
she said & he held her close
& said as far as he was
concerned she was always
that way & her eyes glowed
softly in the light of
his desire

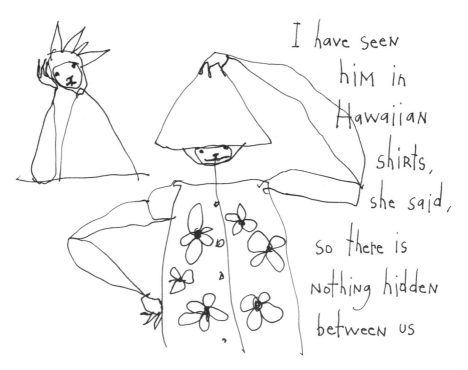

I have seen
him in
Hawaiian
shirts,
she said,
so there is
nothing hidden
between us

Overdressed

good at delegating anxiety

so nobody sleeps all

that well around here

**You see me better
than I am, she said
& I'm worried what'll
happen when your
vision changes**

ready to ride as soon as they decide whether
they want to go in the direction they're all facing

or whether
that'd be
too easy

I'm just going to hide here in
this paper bag until death comes,
she said.

It could be a long time, I said.
There was a pause & then her
head popped out.

You think I should have a hobby
while I wait? she said.

Hobby

Time stands
still best
in moments
that look
suspiciously
like ordinary
life.

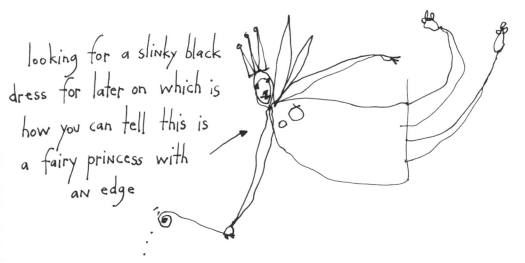

looking for a slinky black
dress for later on which is
how you can tell this is
a fairy princess with
an edge

Ordinary Life

I'm on my way to the future, she said & I said, But you're just sitting there listening & she smiled & said, It's harder than you'd think with all the noise everyone else is making.

Map of some places not discovered quite yet because when people get too close it stands up & trots away

Listening for the Future

Sometimes I can't wait to leave,
but not when my boys are

wishing I could stay

There has never been
a day when I have not
been proud of you,
I said to my son,

though some days
I'm louder about
other stuff so it's
easy to miss that.

Quiet Pride

One Halloween, my sister made a magic wand & she went around giving wishes to all my friends, but when she got glitter on all the candy they yelled at her & she went home crying & later on my mom made me share my candy with her & she was so happy she flung glitter all over & gave me an extra wish I know didn't work because I still have a sister who loves shiny stuff.

Shiny Stuff

torn between wanting to stay & wanting to go
& worried it will be   the wrong decision
                                either way

I asked her what she planned
to do with her life & she said
she was way beyond that
point already. I'm just happy
I remember to be there when
it happens, she said.

has found the real problem with
Post-it notes is
that they don't
stick in your
head

Life Plan

I don't mind dancing with you, he
told her one night, as long as
I get to pick the dance
sometimes.

OK, she said, you pick

so they went home & made popcorn
& looked at magazines all night long

quiet
dance
in heartbeat
time

I saw them standing there pretending to be just friends, when all the time in the world could not pry them apart

this looks like swing dancing but really
it's just moving around the floor
trying not to bump into anybody else

Just Friends

I've seen too many movies
to believe this would happen
to me, he said & she smiled
& kissed him lightly & said,
It's good to let reality in
now & then, don't you think?

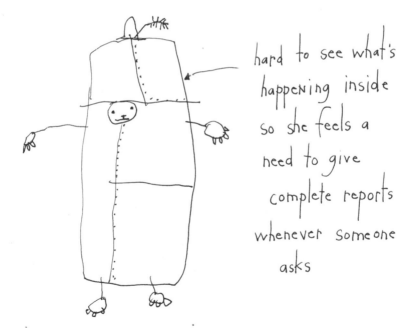

hard to see what's
happening inside
so she feels a
need to give
complete reports
whenever someone
asks

Reality Check

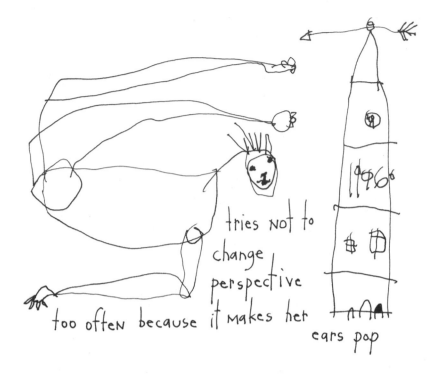

tries not to
change
perspective
too often because it makes her
ears pop

I'll bet you wouldn't even
miss me if I died, she said.
Depends on if you'd been
grumpy in those final days,
I said & she tried to look
sad but I saw the smile
anyway.

Final Days

I'm an outsider
by choice, she
said, but I'm
hoping that won't
be my choice
forever.

this is a machine that
takes your life & does
all the hard parts &
leaves you all the parts
you enjoy & almost
everyone discovers they're
not the parts you'd think
they were at first glance

Outsider

When I was younger, I used to
fly a lot in my dreams. I used to
dream I was naked, too. My grandma
said it was all because of original
sin & that if I lived a pure life
that someday I would be able to
fly naked with Jesus & then she
looked at me & said many are
called, but few are chosen & later
on I thought it was a damn good
thing, too & I gave up pure living
for a long time after that just
to be sure.

Frostbite

likes her body a lot,
especially the way she
can fling it all around
in all sorts of directions
& it still stays connected
in one piece

I've always liked
the time before
dawn because there's
no one around to
remind me who I'm
supposed to be so it's
easier to remember,
who I am.

Before Dawn

I'm not that good at being
a tourist because I'm always
looking at the way the light
shines in your hair or the way
your dress opens to the wind
& my favorite places in the
world are places filled with
you.

Map of all the places you'll
find around here if you put
in enough effort & are
willing to travel using only
your sense of
touch

Can I count on you to be there, no matter what? she said & I said no & she said What kind of friend are you? & I said the kind who won't lie to you any time you want & I think she kept me around as a curiosity after that

When I first met her
I knew in a moment
I would have to spend
the next few days
re-arranging my mind
so there'd be room
for her to stay.

Making Room

I don't think about sex as much as I used to, I said. But all it takes is a little reminder.

Like what? she said.

You name it, I said & I knew instantly I had lost all credibility.

It's lucky I have only one of these, he said.

I can see where you'd never think about anything else.

Do you make all this stuff up on your own? she said
& I said I had a lot of people working for me day
& night & almost none of them knew it & I'm sure
she was impressed until she figured out
what I meant
later on

Does everyone around
here pretend they don't
like sex? she said
& I nodded.
O, she said, then we
should probably not
get to be friends,
because I'm going to
have to move soon.

Cold Climate

I leave it to other people to change, she told me.

I spend my time just cultivating vices.

walking with loud gIANt steps while he CAN because he's Already noticed that when you grow up, even if you do keep walking as big as you CAN, you have to be quiet about it, or other people get headAches

BoOM

BoOM

Cultivating Vice

I try not to lie
on days I didn't
get enough sleep,
my sister told me.
It feels good just
to be transparent.

cursed with
an unerring
sense of
directionlessness
even when
things
are
going
well

You know why kids like skeletons? he said & I said I didn't & he said it was because it didn't matter if you were good or bad, you ended up a bunch of bones

& he stopped for a second & then he added, but you don't have to worry, I'll still be good.

I've always thought death was a lot like Christmas, he said. I can't wait to find out if being good the whole time was worth it.

Being Good

One summer night, we took my parents' grill & we put in some sticks & paper & soaked the whole thing in lighter fluid & then my friend turned on his shortwave radio & we listened to some scientist in Houston who was saying where Apollo was at that moment & at the exact time it went over us, we lit the stuff in the grill so the astronauts would look out & see this light & they'd say 'What the hell is that?' & we danced around the pillar of flame & sparks laughing wildly because while the astronauts were out there unlocking the mysteries of the universe, we were back home in Chicago making more of them.

Pillar of Flame

I like this place
best by moonlight,
she told me.

During the
day, it just
looks like
dirt.

SoME
FACTS, But
MaiNLy THE
Best Bits
FRoM TRUe,
But GRiTTY
Books

← doesn't mind carrying a
few choice pieces
of baggage
so she has a
conversation starter
in almost any social
situation

Moonlight

ROAR-
TWO-
THREE- FOUR

really just
wanting to learn
a few fun dance steps,
but try telling that to
all those panic-stricken Japanese

GODZILLA
goes to
FRED ASTAIRE
TOKYO

I see stuff like
this a lot in my
dreams, so I
decided it should
at least be doing
something useful
while I figure out
what it means.

She tapped her fingers
& nothing happened &
she thought she'd lost
her magic, but it had
only changed & it took
her awhile to figure it
out again

this is a magical beast
that holds the secret of
light & shadow in a
safe place in her heart
& when it has been too
long grey, she starts to
dance & laugh & cry & sing
& the sunlight fills her
up & spills in wild abandon
back into the world again

Magic

I'm not that afraid
of death, she said.
I was in the 60's,
so I've already been
through a lot of
stuff I don't
understand.

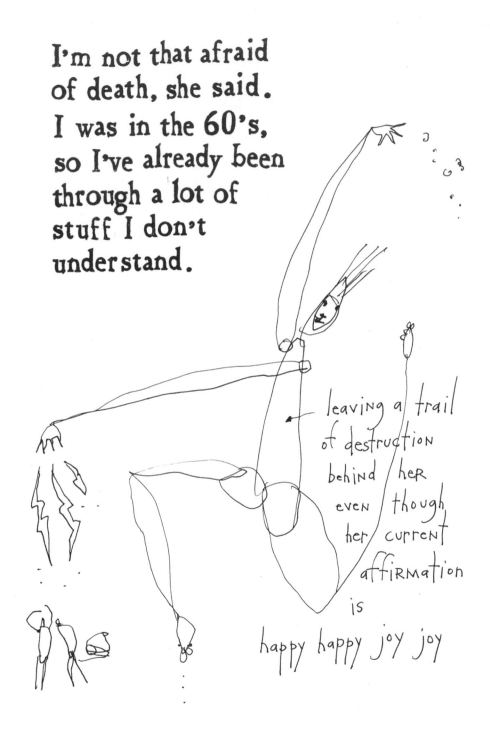

leaving a trail
of destruction
behind her
even though
her current
affirmation
is

happy happy joy joy

Flower Child

this is the exact center of the universe

which explains why None of the usual Rules apply here

What are the rules? I said & he said you run & you run & you run until you fall over. There's a couple others in there for variety, he added, but that's the main one.

Sort of spiritual with a real
fondNess for fAst cars

So of course he
reincarNated as an

AMERiCAN

I'm fastest,
he said, when
I'm the one
that gets
to say go.

oNly half-Naked iN
her dream that Night
because everybody else
was completely naked
& she just had to
be different & when
she woke up, she finally
figured out why she spent Most of
her free time by herself

Advantage

My kids could draw like this, he said
& I said he was lucky they didn't
because I would not wish
children like me on my worst
enemy

& he didn't have   anything
more to say to me

why aren't people dogs?
he said & I said because
we can pick up newspapers
with our hands & that
made sense to him.

It makes sense to make a map of places where you can get eaten by bears, or where there's a bottomless pit, but when you get into making maps of your mind, you're basically wasting your time.

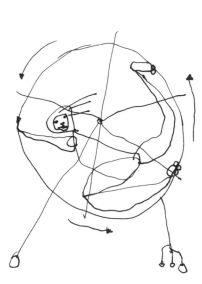

I'm probably best at going where I've already been, she said, but I get bored with it pretty quickly

Mind Map

this is a window into the stuff that goes on
behind what we think about
it & even if we were
all to disappear
tomorrow, it would go
on without even noticing
except to comment
now & then that it was
quieter today than usual

Sometimes I think I should just keep my opinions to myself, she said, but someone has got to be the voice of reason.

Voice of Reason

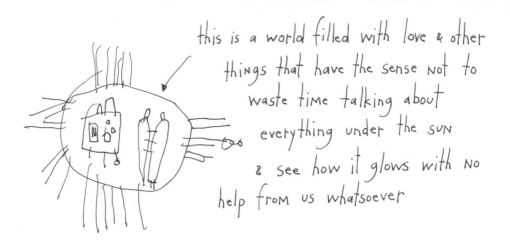

this is a world filled with love & other
things that have the sense not to
waste time talking about
everything under the sun
& see how it glows with no
help from us whatsoever

there came a moment
in the middle of the
song when he suddenly
felt every heartbeat
in the room & after
that he never forgot
he was part of something
much bigger

someone asked them
to be quiet, so it's
just a matter of
time before all
hell breaks loose

Connection

I wish you could have
been there for the sun
& the rain & the long,
hard hills. For the sound
of a thousand conversations
scattered along the road.
For the people laughing &
crying & remembering at
the end.

But, mainly, I wish you
could have been there.

I knew a man in college who grew up in the
inner city of Chicago & what he was doing in Iowa
I never did figure out. But whenever he
would see a jet trailing across the sky, he
would stop everything he was doing & he
would watch. Once, after a jet was gone
& there was nothing left but the white
line disappearing like a scar into the blue,
he turned to me & said, An airplane is
a miracle & I didn't give it much thought,
but now & then, when I am ready to give
up hope for human beings in general, & for
one or two of them who are bugging me
specifically. I will look to the sky & there
will be one of those miracles & I will
remember it's all about concentrating on
the right thing.

Flight

There are things you do
because they feel right
& they may make no sense
& they may make no money
& it may be the real reason
we are here : to love each
other & to eat each other's
cooking & say it was good.

I don't really like
coffee, she said,
but I don't really
like it when my
head hits my desk
when I fall asleep
either

I read once that the
ancient Egyptians had
fifty words for sand
& the Eskimos had a
hundred words for snow.
I wish I had a thousand
words for love, but all
that comes to mind is
the way you move against
me while you sleep

& there are no words
for that.

No Words

thinks of aerobics with the fondness of someone who has decided it is a chapter now closed in her life

These are 'little scraps of magic & when you paste them together you get a memory of something fine & strong, she said. Sometimes it takes till you're a lot older to see it though.

this is a machine that's supposed to make civilization, but it's only theoretical because it takes a lot more civilization than we've got at the moment to get it to work

Scraps of Magic

The two of them went riding off into the future one day when they ran into a group of old people out looking for roots & when they stopped to see if they could help, all the old people laughed & said they had no business heading into the future until they had more experience.

One woman said the future wasn't even there except for the bad parts, because the future's always worse than before & then the old people left, walking slowly, shouting at each other about the weather.

The two of them looked at each other for a minute & then they said, let's go off to the future again & before they left they made a rule to keep on the lookout for old people.

On the Lookout

leaning out as far
as she CAN, hoping
she'll fALL SOON

So she can
stop worrying
about whether
it will
happen
or not.

Hoping to Fall

A lot of people think he's kind of formless but it's only because they keep hoping he'll look like something they recognize before they get too anxious

The future is a funny thing, she told me one day, because we're the only ones who care about it.

this is a picture of the future & you'll notice that there's a lot of blank space because people haven't made up their minds about it & the future doesn't have a lot of time for that kind of indecisiveness

Careless Future

I'm very broad minded
usually, she said, but it
gets very narrow & fast
in spots.

this is
a secret
potion that
makes you
see the world
differently
& she's found
it safest to
use only on the
weekends

Life must be cheaper here, she said & I said I don't think life is cheap anywhere, but there are some places people haven't added it up yet because they're too busy making stuff for America.

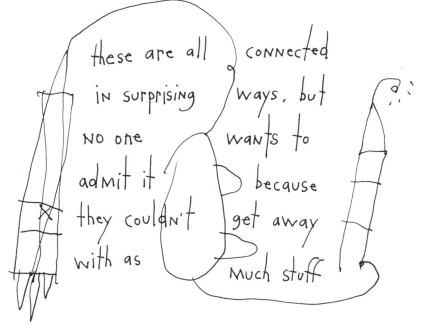

these are all connected in surprising ways, but no one wants to admit it because they couldn't get away with as much stuff

He said who invented evil?
& I said I wasn't sure anybody
invented it, it just happened
when somebody got tired of
all the effort it took to live
right.

They probably didn't have
anyone to teach them, he said
& I thought to myself, we
might be doing this right
after all.

I don't really like dogs, my uncle told me once, but it's a good way to keep up with what's going on in the neighborhood

Does it count as gossip, she said, if you just know those people would go & do something like that?

Certain types of people don't fit in here, she told me when we first moved in.

Just assume you're one of them & you'll be fine.

Expect the Worst

He said being
invisible wasn't
so bad except
when you're
trying to get
quick service.

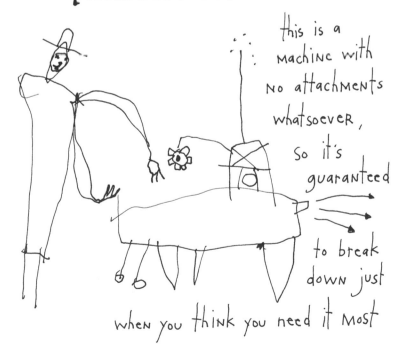

this is a
machine with
no attachments
whatsoever,
so it's
guaranteed
to break
down just
when you think you need it most

travelling as fast in one direction as she can go before she has second thoughts & goes back to doing the same old stuff

I do much better as a goddess, she said, since my secretarial skills have always been limited.

this is a talking bird puppet & it usually has a lot to say after she's been on another bad date

Goddess

I think I'm having a heart
attack, she said, but it's
dragging on for hours.

I told her not to worry.
That's how most people
who work a full day
feel, I said.

everybody's
dancing in place
because they
don't want to
mess up the house
since it just
got cleaned

Full Day

He only gets vicious when
he watches too much tv,
so we keep public radio
on most of the time
instead

Box filled
with free
gifts that
you listen to
only after
there's nothing
else to do

so mainly
all we have to
worry about is him going around
to all the neighbors asking for money.

RULES FOR A SUCCESSFUL HOLIDAY
1. GET together WITH the FAMILY
2. RELIVE OLD TIMES
3. GET OUT BEFORE IT BLOWS.

I try & walk a line between
terror, & ecstasy, she said &
then she shook her head.
You'd be amazed at the people
who avoid me for, no good
reason, other than that.

He just sat in the
church looking up at
nothing in particular
& I whispered what
are you doing? & he
said if Jesus had been
a chicken would we
have Weber grills all
over the place instead
of crosses? & I had a
hard time concentrating
after that, too.

Why do they treat us like
children? they said & I
said why do you treat them
like adults?

    & their eyes opened wide &
they began to laugh & talk all
at once & suddenly everything
looked possible again

trying to remember when it
stopped being theory & turned
into REAL LIFE, because
theory was a whole lot
    easier

Equal Treatment

this is an invitation
to an amazing future

& I can guarantee it
because most futures
are

& even if they aren't
there are better things
to do than blaming me
about it

this is a machine that's supposed to
make people good & true & kind & the
funny thing is that it works best when
it's completely broken down so everyone
has to stop what they're doing
& get together & figure out how to
fix it

Invitation to a Future

Someday, the light will
shine like a sun through
my skin & they will say,
What have you done with
your life? & though there
are many moments I think
I will remember, in the
end, I will be proud to say,
I was one of us.

About the Artist

Brian Andreas is a fiber artist, sculptor, and storyteller. He uses traditional media from fine art, theatre, and storytelling, as well as electronic media, to explore new ways of being an artist. He also likes to put things together with the rustiest stuff he can find. His work is shown and collected internationally.

Born in 1956 in Iowa City, Iowa, he holds a B.A. from Luther College in Decorah, Iowa, and an M.F.A. in Fiber and Mixed Media from John F. Kennedy University in Orinda, California.

After spending the last few years in Iowa, he and his family are now on the move again, still not quite knowing where they're going to end up when the dust settles (but secure in the knowledge that it will have great restaurants...)

About StoryPeople

StoryPeople are wood sculptures, three to four feet tall, in a roughly human form. They can be as varied as a simple cutout figure, or an assemblage of found and scrap wood, or an intricate, roughly made treasure box. Each piece uses only recycled barn and fence wood from old homesteads in the northeast Iowa area. Adding to their individual quirkiness are scraps of old barn tin and twists of wire. They are painted with bright colors and hand-stamped a letter at a time (using the same stamp set that you see on the hand-stamped pages of this book), with original stories. The most striking aspect of StoryPeople are the shaded spirit faces. These faces are softly blended into the wood surface, and make each StoryPerson come alive.

Every figure is marked and numbered at the studio, and is unique because of the materials used. The figures, the colorful story prints, and the books, are available in galleries and stores throughout the US, Canada and the UK (along with a few others scattered about the world), and on our web site. Please feel free to call or write for more information, or drop in on the web at **www.storypeople.com**

StoryPeople
P.O. Box 7
Decorah, IA 52101
USA

800.476.7178
319.382.8060
319.382.0263 FAX

orders@storypeople.com